Benedict

Stories of the Great Saint

Retold by Norvene Vest
Pictures by Father Maur

SOURCE BOOKS TRABUCO CANYON CALIFORNIA

Library of Congress Cataloging–in–Publication Data
Vest, Norvene.
    Benedict: stories of the great saint / retold by Nor-
vene Vest: pictures by Fr. Maur.
        p.   cm.
Summary: A biography of the medieval monk, St. Benedict,
adapted from the writings of Pope Gregory.
ISBN 0-940147-43-2 (pbk.)
1. Benedict, Saint, Abbot of Monte Cassino--juvenile literature.
2. Christian saints--Italy--Biography--Juvenile literature.
I. Gregroy I. Pope, ca 540-604. Benedictus.
II. Doorslaer, Muar-Etienne van, ill. III. Title.
BR1720.B45V47 1997
27t'. 102--dc21
[B]   97-6703
                                           CIP AC

ISBN 0-940147-43-2

Published by:

Source Books
PO Box 794
Trabuco Canyon CA 92678

Printed and bound by Patterson Printing, Benton Harbor, MI, USA

This book is dedicated to my mother, in thanksgiving for your many gifts to me, not least of which are your courage and love;

to Mary Rose, who keeps urging me to tell the stories;

and to Fr. Abbot Francis Benedict and Fr. Maur-Etienne van Doorslaer for Fr. Maur's wonderful sketches of Benedict's life which grace this book.

PREFACE

S AINT BENEDICT LIVED IN Italy not long
after the great military victory of the Germanic tribes in Rome, which is sometimes
called 'The Fall of Rome.' Only two records of
his life exist, one of which is the great Rule he
wrote, and the other is a narrative of his
miracles written shortly after his death by
Pope Gregory. I have put the stories in the
voice of Gregory himself: after all, it is really
he who is telling the stories about his spiritual
father. The stories here are adapted from
Gregory's book, and they also include many
ideas which come from Benedict's Rule.

When we think of a rule, we may imagine
a rigid standard, but what is meant in this case
is something more like a measuring-stick, a
ruler, an aid to help us know that we are on the
right track. Benedict's Rule was remarkably

flexible and adaptable, so that not only was it useful throughout the Middle Ages, but it is still used today in all parts of the world. Indeed, from Benedict's death in 540, until around 1600, it was the basic governing document for communities of women and men through all Europe.

If you visit a monastery, you can expect to find people still living life very much as Benedict outlined it. When they wake up each day, they pray and listen to God in the early hours, then have breakfast and go to whatever is their work. From time to time during the day, the monastics come together again for short prayers (called 'offices'), and then they remember God again at the end of their workday and before bedtime.

Generally, the community has a meal after every major time of prayer, and often guests can join them in both prayer and food. The monastery with which I am affiliated is St. Andrew's Abbey in Valyermo, California, and they have a special retreat center for youth as well as adults, so everyone is welcome.

Communities of men are known as monasteries, and if a man lives separately and alone for a time, he is called a hermit. Women's communities may be called monasteries or convents, and sometimes women are called nuns, or consecrated virgins. Today we often use the general term 'monastic' to apply both to men and women who have dedicated their lives to God in this way. Also, married people like myself, who do not actually live in a monastery, may choose to commit themselves to the Benedictine way as much as possible, and we are called 'oblates.'

I hope you enjoy getting to know Benedict through these stories, and that you want to find out more by seeking out some Benedictines near you. God bless you.

NORVENE VEST, ALTADENA, 1997

IN THE CAVE AT EASTER

Y OU KNOW HE WAS a great man. His monastery at Monte Cassino (where I served) was truly a blessed Christian community. But he did not come by his greatness easily. He often told the novices tales about his early years, and of his mistakes and failures. He gave us courage by telling us frankly about the problems he confronted, and how God helped him overcome them. How honest he was, and how unfailingly gentle! He learned wisdom the way most of us do—through trial and error, surrender and gift.

How did it all begin? He was a twin, you know, born with his sister Scholastica in a small town in northern Italy, called Norcia. Their father was on the town council, and the family was modestly well off, but the times were not any easier then than they are now. When the twins' father was a child, the barbarians who now rule us, invaded Rome, and the lands of the Empire fell deeper into decline. Such inflation and corruption we suffer now, and so many homeless poor and ill people!

When he was sixteen, Benedict was sent here to Rome for what is called 'advanced education.' He studied grammar, arithmetic, geometry, history and astronomy. His tutors specialized in public speaking and writing, emphasizing style and diction. Benedict's old nurse found an apartment for them in the city, and he would walk to a nearby storefront school before dawn, and was free to wander around the city by the early afternoon. Once a week there was a holiday, because the open-air markets were set up in the streets and it was too noisy for lessons. Benedict attended one of the many magnificent Roman churches at least once a week, but he was distressed by feuding congregations and the various papal factions.

At first, Benedict had been in awe of Rome, with its huge palaces and fine houses, many covered with thin slabs of marble which shone in the sun. But he soon noticed the decay everywhere. Statues and temples which once had been grand and imposing structures were beginning to crumble, and the flats where ordinary people lived frequently caught on fire. Narrow streets were rutted and strewn with waste left from shops or thrown from upstairs windows. For a fresh country boy like Benedict, it was just too much!

Benedict could never really fit in here. The constant noise and traffic bothered him, but I think even more than these, he was upset by what he called the 'moral fiber' of the people. It sounds old-fashioned these days. But we know what he meant: people were more at ease with little white lies than with honesty, and public orators seemed to value style more than truth. Students were more interested in personalities and parties than in solid study, and teachers found technical details safer than genuine curiosity. Among the citizens of Rome there was a general boredom interrupted occasionally by frantic activity—both masking an underlying despair. Sometimes the ever-present violence seemed a perverse effort just to feel alive. All the games and festivals and spectacles concocted for the arena came and went, but could not fill the void. Numb, people clamored continuously for escalating excitement.

Benedict was revolted by all of it, and after several years, without finishing his schooling, he just left. I am sure you can imagine the outraged idealism he felt: fearless, headstrong, impatient, sure he could do better at this business of living than any of the adults he knew.

Fed up with people, Benedict decided it was God alone he wanted. He took a few precious scrolls of scripture and a blanket to sleep in, and found a cave. A discreet old monk brought him a little food every week, and Benedict withdrew from the populated world. He stayed in that cave for three years.

I have often wondered what that time was like, for in later years Benedict seldom spoke of it, yet it must have shaped the rest of his life. His only company in that long time was the great silence, a little scripture, and God.

You can still visit that cave at Subiaco, high on the steep mountain. Dark, rocky soil and heavy brush almost obscure the entrance. You can barely make out the ceiling above in the darkness. Benedict had a little oil lamp for light, but he used it sparingly. Yet the rocky walls appear almost iridescent; they pulse with a presence that makes me want to fall on my knees.

Away from all the distractions of ordinary life, young Benedict came face to face with himself. Thinking back over his life, he began to see more clearly his own greed and lust and pride, perhaps more subtly expressed, but so the more dangerous for his soul. While he had been critical of others' extravagance, he realized how much of his own he had taken for granted. Judging the dishonesty of others, he found himself gossiping about them. In the silence of his own cave, Benedict realized that he could never flee his society altogether, as though he were somehow not part of it. For good or bad, he shared the weaknesses and compulsions of his time. He no longer saw 'the others' as the foulness from which he longed to escape to his own purity. At first, this realization only made him pray harder: was his task in that cave to repent for himself and for everyone else too?

In time, however, the luminous presence of God in the cave, stole through Benedict's concentration on sin. Month after month, he lived a life of lenten penitence, in poverty and discipline trying to purge his soul of every desire. But occasionally he was caught by surprise in a moment of purest gladness.

One evening he was sitting just inside the cave as sunset filled the sky across the valley, and his cypress trees were penetrated with reds and golds. Gazing at the sight, Benedict felt his heart would burst with joy. In the moment he knew nothing at all except a swelling sense of utter completeness; afterwards he marveled that it seemed God was massaging open his heart, enlarging it so it could receive the fullness of God's very being.

The young monk would experience occasional nudges such as this. Then one day they developed into a crisis. Something very odd happened. A neighboring monk deliberately made his way up to Benedict's cave with a picnic basket on his arm. Usually Benedict saw no-one and if he did, he avoided conversation. But this old man had come a long way and wanted to talk, and Benedict humored him. At last, the monk said: "Brother, I've brought a picnic lunch which I urge you to share." Benedict pulled back at once, piously

explaining that he lived a life of penitence and was fasting as usual. The monk protested: "But, my friend, today is Easter Day!"

Benedict never forgot that moment, later speaking of it many times. Suddenly he saw that emphasis on sin can hold God away. His prayer had centered on his limitations rather than on God's generosity. In solitude he forgot that Lent is intended to prepare for Holy Easter with joy and spiritual longing. He had been living with the Cross but not the Resurrection!

The insight overwhelmed him: what Easter means is that *the world is God's*. And the God he knew, that tender and loving presence in his cave, was also out in the world, alongside the whole human family. Well, he laughed aloud, and sat down and ate that picnic lunch with relish.

Later, when I knew Abbot Benedict, he was a man possessed by a profound sense of being loved. He never spoke of this directly, but you could not miss it in him. Maybe the love embarrassed him for he always made clear that he knew he did not *deserve* it. But he also insisted that he had no right to *refuse* what God had longed to give, and he urged us to see that too. I can only describe this quality of presence in Benedict as humility mixed with exaltation. He was a man of deep and warm conviction: no sin ever shocked him, but he thought it far more important that each of us is daily invited to receive God in our hearts, to be transformed in love. What mattered most to him was God's vibrant love always and everywhere.

Benedict lived to celebrate God's presence in and with others, and to watch that presence flowing out into everything! He was himself a continual YES to God. It was splendid to behold, and a great gift to me: learning to notice and delight in God, in Christ everywhere, and to live centered in that reality.

A BIRD IN DISGUISE

M ONTHS LATER, THE LOCAL villagers discovered Benedict's cave. It happened
this way. A goat had followed her kid halfway
up the mountain before the goatherd realized
that they had wandered off. When the young
goatherd climbed up to rescue the baby and
its mother, he almost stumbled over Benedict
praying under an olive tree. The goatherd was
even more surprised than Benedict—he had
not imagined that anyone lived up there—but
he liked the hermit immediately and proposed
to come back again and talk.

A month later, the goatherd returned in
the mid-morning and shyly asked Benedict to
tell him the meaning of a mural in the church,
showing Jesus with a lamb on his shoulders.
Almost before the young man knew it, the day
had passed in talk of God, and the sun was

setting. As he hurried home, the goatherd's thoughts were filled with memories of the holy man who lived in the cliffs.

Of course, he told his family and his fellows, and gradually more people found their way up the mountain to seek out Benedict. They appreciated the way he listened carefully and then helped them see how God was working in their own lives. After talk with Benedict, the villagers felt that they had been in God's presence too, and they returned home with glad hearts.

But later, Abbot Benedict confessed to us novices that those visits created a serious problem for him. He knew about the idea of spiritual pride, of course, but personally he had not yet been tested in it. With all those people praising him, before he quite knew what was happening, Benedict began to think of himself as a holy man, believing that he was extraordinary. He started watching his words, and imagining people lauding him in his biography.

He was captured by his own image of himself. Later he would confess that he had been aspiring to be holy before he really was.

How strange that a man we now think of as holy was actually tempted with the idea of becoming holy! It almost seems that thinking too much about spiritual progress prevents spiritual maturity. Still, I think one expression of holiness is a willingness to notice our weaknesses and offer them to God, asking to be changed. Benedict told us that sometimes a little humiliation helps us to notice our limitations, and he got a good lesson in humiliation from, of all things, a little blackbird.

He was sitting in the sun, one winter day, reading from his precious scripture scrolls, when he was disturbed by an insistent noise in a nearby thornbush. A throaty *krruck, krruk* burst continuously from the beak of a small blackbird perched on an overhead branch. As Benedict turned his head to observe the little bird, the creature flew to a closer perch, and called out again, *krruck, krruk!* At first Benedict tried to ignore it, but the bird demanded notice. As it flew up near Benedict with wings and tail spread, the monk threw up his hands in exasperation to ward off the bird. Just as he managed to refocus his attention on his reading, the call started up again, *krruck, krruk!* Irritation pushed away Benedict's peace. What a nuisance! His study and prayer with scripture was important. How annoying that this upstart blackbird did not sense his blessedness and glide quietly away, leaving him to his holy work! Benedict jumped up and vigorously waved the bird away.

Benedict's blissful concentration on holy matters was totally gone. The moment the blackbird was out of sight, he felt the irritation rising through his chest and throat, flushing his cheeks and even causing a ringing in his ears. Anger constricted his lungs, and he gasped, unable to get his breath. How dare that bird interrupt his precious solitude and disturb his meditation time! Curse that bird. What *was* the evil spirit that could remain even in the absence of the bird itself? Perhaps the bird's black form was merely a disguise for the devil himself, come to tempt Benedict.

Even as the idea of temptation came to mind, Benedict's emotions shifted to guilt that he had allowed himself to be distracted by a simple bird. He knew that birds are neither good nor evil, and even the smallest sparrow is within God's care. Now his anger and blame shifted focus to his own unworthiness. If indeed he was such a holy man, after so many months of practice, he should be able to remain serenely in prayerful study, no matter what the distraction. Benedict mentally cursed himself now, feeling utterly a failure. He was such a fraud. Perhaps he should leave the monastic life altogether.

Just the thought of leaving allowed his mind to fill with images of all he had given up to come to this cave. Memories crowded in—

15

of a beautiful woman he once knew, of the fine home where his tutor lived, of his gifts of eloquence and intelligence which he had buried in his present simplicity. Now he bitterly regretted losing all those things and abandoning his career in its prime. He longed for something he could call his own—a wife and children, fine furnishings, an elegant chariot— at that moment even a well-made writing stylus would have comforted him. Having given up everything, he was left with nothing at all! Benedict wept now in self-pity.

In just a few seconds, the hermit moved through the range of emotions: from pride to guilt to despair. He began to beat himself with accusations: he had only imagined that God had called him to the cave; he helped others mainly because he needed to be needed; he was wasting his life in the illusion that prayer could make a difference. He found himself crying aloud, "Oh, Lord, I am a fool and a failure, and might as well die!"

Krruck, krruk! The blackbird was back. Was it the little bird's fault that Benedict found himself awash in a sea of emotion, prey to the temptation to abandon his monastic life? At first, Benedict had imagined it was the blackbird's spirit which drew him 'outside himself,' cutting him off from a sense of God's presence. Certainly *something* had tempted Benedict, had pulled him away from his usual center in Christ. His emotions and thoughts had tugged him against his will into a pool of doubt and despair. But now, at the reassuring immediacy of the bird's insistent call, Benedict was brought back into the concreteness of the present moment. He remembered that far stronger than any temptation was the constant presence of the Lord God. If the creature was really in God's care, might it not be bringing a message from God's very self?

The monk watched the bird with new attention. The blackbird was perched again on the thorn bush, contentedly going about its business, in the protective thorns. Benedict was astonished at how noisy the bird was. It sang loudly as it hopped along a limb and shuffled boldly in the leaves looking for caterpillars; it had no fear at all. The bird even courted attention, naturally trusting in God's care in the thorn shelter, and in its own strong wings. Instinctively, the bird was fully itself, and fully relying on God, at one and the same time.

Watching God's creature, Benedict gave a deep sigh, releasing the tension he had been holding in his body. He breathed deeply again, it felt so good. Did not the scripture say that the Spirit was the breath of God? Every time he breathed, he was depending on God's Spirit for life itself. A third time, Benedict breathed deeply. God cared for him no less than he cared for the little birds. He knew that even now, God was loving him very much, not because of anything Benedict did, but because God had made him.

Benedict realized it was his own fault that he felt temptation. If, in the first place, he had not succumbed to an exaggerated view of himself, he would not have been susceptible to danger. He exalted himself and sought marvel beyond him, pretending that holiness belonged to him rather than to God abiding in his heart. Pride had made its home in him, and brought Brother Despair for company, both being different faces of the same distorted self-image. The blackbird's message to Benedict was an invitation to be who he really was: not someone puffed up with pride, but a man dependent upon the love of God. Yet just because of God's love, he was also not to be cast down with despair. Hope always endures through the abundant mercy of God.

You can imagine how astonished we novices were to hear our abbot speaking years later about his limitations and vulnerability. But how clearly he showed us the importance of a humble confession of the heart's secrets, even though they might sting like nettles. Those stinging nettles are transformed through openness, into protective thorns, within whose shelter we can be genuinely ourselves.

Benedict was a man who lived immersed in that perfect love of God which casts out fear. He never again cursed a bird, and indeed was ever after blessed by them. From that day, Benedict set out to serve God by serving others, even knowing that he was inadequate for the task. He did his best, and trusted in God for the rest.

He even told us that during his long life he never did feel that he loved and trusted God as fully as he longed to, (imagine that!) but that he knew God called him to the work anyway. Every day of his life, he asked God to purify the fire of his pride and melt the ice of his despair. And that was more than enough. Benedict discovered what he went to the cave to find: that his own life was hid with Christ in God.

SAVED

EVEN WITH THE INCREASE in visitors, Benedict continued to live as a hermit in his cave, but he gained a special companion. One day, Benedict noticed a young raven, not more than six months old, just standing on a ledge above the cave. When he noticed that the raven fledgling had not moved the next day, or the next, he realized that it must have become separated from its family and was injured.

Slowly working his way up the cliff face, Benedict captured the bird and brought it back to his cave, where he fed it a mash of bread and water while it regained strength. The raven was very docile, mostly from hunger and exposure, although it might have sustained a concussion in the hailstorm a few days before. Benedict tenderly cared for the little raven, feeding it by hand several times a

day, and it was not long before the man and
the bird were inseparable. As the raven grew
stronger, it would fly far away to seek food in
the daytime, but it always would return to the
cave well before sundown.

One morning after the raven had flown off,
Benedict received a large delegation of monks.
It seems the abbot of their nearby monastery
of Vicovaro had died. Having heard of
Benedict's holiness, the whole community had
made the trek up to his cave to ask him to be
their new superior. Benedict asked for a week
to pray on their request before giving them an
answer.

That evening, the raven returned to find
the hermit in intense prayer. It cocked its dark
head as if to inquire what could be so serious
a matter. As Benedict prayed on the request of
the Vicovaro monks, he came to feel that he
should say 'no.' Perhaps he sensed he was not
ready. Certainly, from the little he had heard
about Vicovaro's easy-going practices, the

match between his own spiritual path and that of the monastery was a poor one.

When the monks returned a week later, Benedict declined their offer. However, they refused to accept his decision, and they spent the whole day working to change his mind. In the end, their sheer persistence prevailed, and Benedict agreed. The raven returned at dusk only to find the Vicovaro monks escorting him along the way to their monastery, a few miles distant. In distress, the bird flew after them, hoarsely crying *kraaak!* in solemn warning.

Sometimes nowadays when we think of the Saints, we imagine they had no faults, no inner struggles, and always did God's will perfectly on the first try—in short, that they were quite unlike ourselves! Benedict would have been appalled that anyone might think such things about him; he knew himself to be an ordinary human being with his own blind spots and frailties. Later, when he told us this story, he always emphasized that it clearly revealed his own failure. Without doubt, there were others who were also responsible for things going so badly astray, but he knew he had made the troubles worse. He gladly shared his failures, to help us discover how better to handle our own.

Well, Benedict went to Vicovaro, convinced that what the monks needed was a tough new regime. He had been taught that progress in the spiritual life was won by rigid discipline. At that time, serious monks fasted all day, every day. They spoke rarely, spent many nights in wakeful vigil, and owned nothing at all. (One fellow in Egypt was famous because of his discipline of sitting for days in discomfort, alone atop a stone column).

So, Benedict set out to take forceful control, eager to establish his authority right away. He imposed a single standard of life on everyone, not allowing for the natural ebb and flow of grace in every life, nor for diversity of individual needs. It was only much later that Benedict thought about the great contrast between the beginning of his relationship with the raven, which was tender and caring, and the beginning of his relationship with the monks at Vicovaro, which was rigid and uncompromising.

For their part, the monks at Vicovaro genuinely admired the quality of life they had seen in Benedict from afar, but they disliked intensely living under his direction. Instead of yielding to his demands, they hardened in their waywardness. When the new abbot dictated a diet of only raw food, they raided the nearby beehives for extra honey. If Benedict insisted on silence day and night, they invented obscene hand-signs to pass among themselves when his back was turned. They grumbled continuously at Benedict's strange ways, which they rightly saw as standing in criticism of them, and their resentment grew: after all, they had lived comfortably enough as monks for some time before this young up-start came to join them. They fiercely regret-ted choosing Benedict as their abbot. But what could they do? There was no way to get rid of an abbot; once they had selected him he was theirs for life.

Of course, those monks of Vicovaro were refusing God's invitation to them. They were acting like the ungodly men of the Book of Wisdom, or the Pharisees in Jesus' time, in-viting their own death by the errors of their lives. But later Benedict would confess that he had also badly erred. He had isolated himself mentally, forgetting his own frailty, and let-ting judgment triumph over mercy in his atti-tude towards his charges. He tried to purge the evil out of the monks by his own hand, rather than to lead them firmly but gently into the healing presence of God. He had set out to be feared rather than loved.

Well—you can guess the result! Instead of eliminating their evil ways, the abbot presented a target for them: himself! Instead of helping the monks toward a deeper exploration of their own motives and desires, Benedict's rigidity made it easy for them to pretend the problem belonged entirely to someone else. The monks thought that if only they could get rid of Benedict, everything would be fine again. They took desperate measures. Poison.

Benedict had awoken early that day with his raven. It was their custom to rise early together, Benedict from his pallet and the raven from its roost. They would meet at a pool of water, where Benedict would splash his face, and the raven hopped around the shallow edges, wetting its feathers. When both had drunk a little, Benedict would pray as the raven preened and gently set his feathers in place. Normally, the raven flew of for its day's foraging when Benedict joined the community for morning prayers.

But on this particular day, the senior monks had risen much earlier than their abbot. Indeed, they had been up most of the night, plotting how to kill Benedict. One had obtained a pouch of poisoned herbs, which another had ground into a fine powder. A third monk had purchased a strong wine for the mid-day meal, and had thoroughly mixed it with the poison in the pitcher for Benedict's table. The monks had been unusually jittery at the morning offices, but Benedict had long since ceased attending to their passing moods. In absolute silence Abbot Benedict walked from the chapel to the refectory, and took his place at the head of the table.

One of the very junior monks, not knowing what the seniors were up to, carried the abbot's pitcher to his table and held it for his blessing. But just as he was making the sign of the Cross over it, the raven unexpectedly flew through the doorway, straight for Benedict's head. The startled abbot jumped, and the pitcher fell and shattered. The dismayed monks saw the pitcher of poisoned wine break at Benedict's upraised hand of blessing, as if struck with a stone!

Not long afterwards, a jealous neighboring priest named Florentius tried again to poison the abbot, perhaps inspired by the disgruntled monks. Florentius sent Abbot Benedict a poisoned loaf of bread, but again, Benedict's friend the raven wrecked the plot. Benedict usually started his light evening meal by sharing his bread with the raven on its return from the day's foraging. On this occasion, when Benedict set the loaf in front of the bird, it began to jump up and down squawking its *kwaak!* in great disturbance. The raven circled the bread, approaching and retreating, mumbling to itself. Benedict heeded the warning, and told the raven to fly far away with the bread, allowing no-one to eat it. Astonished, the monks watched the raven fly right outside with the loaf, and that was the last anyone saw of the poisoned food. In the middle of the night they heard the weary bird return and Benedict set some water and food before it, praising the creature's courage and love.

The next morning, Benedict and the raven left Vicovaro and returned to their home in the Subiaco heights. The troubled monks were terrified of Benedict's mysterious protection, but at least they had lifted his burdensome yoke from their shoulders.

Benedict reflected long and hard on what had happened at Vicovaro. Clearly, the loving care of the raven had saved him from a terrible death, not once but twice. But what had happened to bring things to such a state that men should try to poison him? When he spoke of the matter to us, he confessed his guilt and remorse; he knew that he had not been wise enough to seek the face of Christ in those who offered their obedience to him. He had seen only their mistakes, and had been blind to their genuine yearning for God.

When Benedict had found the fledgling raven, its helplessness had immediately drawn him to it. Quite naturally he had been compassionate because of the bird's lack of strength, and his love had evoked the loving response of the bird. But with the Vicovaro monks, Benedict's hatred of their faults had seemed to be hatred of the brothers. By rubbing too hard to remove the rust, he almost broke the vessels.

As our abbot, many years later, Benedict was quite a different man. It was hard for us to believe that the events at Vicovaro really had happened, except that Benedict treasured a beautiful black feather, which he said was a sign of how God saved his soul as well as his body. And when the Abbot gazed deeply into my eyes with such love, I had the strange feeling that he saw Christ there, as he did in all my brothers. His sight helped us believe that Christ really did dwell in us, and we yearned to be worthy of that.

LIVING WATER

W HILE BENEDICT REMAINED IN his cave
above Subiaco, his life was changing
radically. Word of his wisdom had reached
Rome, and several noble families had even
asked Benedict to raise their sons in God's
service. Men of all ages gathered around Benedict to learn how to consecrate their lives to
God, and before long twelve communities of
twelve persons each were established throughout the neighboring hills. As overall head of
these monasteries, Benedict gave direction in
practical issues as well as spiritual ones, because everyone knew Christ was served even
in ordinary life decisions.

Three of the monasteries were very high up
in the rocky hills around lake Subiaco, and their
monks regularly journeyed down and back for
water. Tying large jars on their shoulders, they

would pick their way among the crevices, sometimes needing both hands to prevent a fall. On the return trip, the jars were so heavy that only the strongest monks could carry them, and even they had to rest frequently. The task was so difficult and time-consuming that the monks felt it sensible to locate the monasteries elsewhere, and a committee came to see Benedict about a move. Benedict listened carefully, assuring them that he shared their concern. But he never made a decision without prayer, so he asked them to return the next day for his decision.

That night, Benedict went on a long hike— he was still a young man then, and had more energy than I do now! He took a little boy with him by the name of Placid. 'Placid' means 'child of peace.' Together they climbed the steep and dangerous slope, all the way to the top, where separate paths led off to the three monasteries. Even though it was a hard journey, Benedict believed that the Lord often reveals what is better to the younger people, and he needed the gentle child with him in prayer. When they arrived at the top of the slope, Benedict did not make for the monasteries but instead sought a private place nearby to pray. Placid settled himself by a large rock, praying as he could, sleeping as he must, for Benedict's vigil was a long one.

As scripture teaches, Benedict prayed on the mountain through the night: like Moses, alone on mount Sinai for the Hebrew people, and Jesus, struggling in the Garden of Gethsemane on behalf of all God's children. With Benedict, as with Moses and Jesus, the intensity of prayer evoked sweat and tears of anguish.

When the Abbot first told me about that night, I was perplexed. Why should this simple decision call for such intense prayer? My first thought was that the long daily journey for water was good spiritual discipline for the monks, because it involved so much labor and suffering. But Benedict chided me, reminding me that the practical elements of daily life should support prayer, rather than detract from it.

I remember how surprised I was at the first words Benedict told us about morning prayer: he told us to be sure to get a good night's rest, so that our food from the evening meal would be fully digested, and also to take a break shortly after beginning, so that we could heed nature's call for natural elimination! The Abbot always planned not only for our safety, but also for our comfort. You know, it is strange: he stressed that grumbling was a most serious sin against life in community, but equally as abbot he tried hard to arrange things so that we never had reason to grumble. He did not want daily burdens to exceed our strength. In fact, as he matured, Benedict resisted any extremes of discipline, feeling that body, mind, and soul worked best in harmonious movement toward God.

Clearly Benedict would not pretend that such a long and arduous daily journey for water was good for the souls of the monastics; he must have recognized it as a discouraging problem. So then, why not just go ahead and move the monasteries? It was what the monks wanted and it could not be that difficult to do, so why did he not just accept the obvious solution? Why take the time and trouble to struggle all night in prayer? Because Benedict prayed so hard that night, it must have been an especially difficult decision for him. Somehow he sensed that moving the monasteries might be against God's will.

That night as he prayed, Benedict occasionally talked with Placid to help clarify his concern. "What is the first vow of our monks, child?" Placid responded promptly, his knowledge born of his boundless curiosity about the monks' lives.

"Stability, Father."

"Just so, child," Benedict mused. "If I do not find God here, where will I? If I keep wandering, impatient and discontent, I take leave not only of myself, but of God. Stability helps me settle down and lets roots grow deep. If that principle is so important for the committed life, dare I move these monasteries without better reason than this?" After a few such words, Benedict would go back again to his place of prayer, kneeling, and beseeching God.

The cold of the rock seeped through Benedict's thin garment and stole into his protesting muscles. From time to time the abbot glanced over and smiled fondly at the sleeping boy, even as his own mind cried to God for help. He felt a keen sense of being in God's presence as he prayed; the rock atop the mountain was a privileged place of meeting, he was sure.

After a time, the monk stood and walked back and forth on the mountain top. He marveled at the wonders to be seen everywhere, since he had learned to experience God's touch through every created place and thing. See how the stars were tonight in a different position in the sky than a few months ago. What infinite mystery flickered in the single but ever-moving flame of a candle. How quickly and well the recent small cut on Placid's knee had healed! The signs of God's care were revealed everywhere to one with the time and place to watch in awe. Far from being bored with the same old things, Benedict found that every moment revealed a new dimension of God's life. The vow of Stability planted him in God to meet life as it happened.

The sky's darkness seemed to echo the continuing darkness of his mind: he was still unclear about what to do. The problem seemed insoluble: either force the monks to continue an unacceptable level of work for their basic needs, or disrupt the stability of these three monasteries. Benedict saw no way through the darkness, and yet God had surprised him many times before. He returned to his kneeling stone, praying wordlessly from his heart.

As the inky depth of the sky began ever so slightly to lighten, Benedict noticed a new scent in the air. He sniffed, turned his head, and sniffed again. What was it...could it possibly be the scent of water? Here, on the mountain high above the black lake, he suddenly sensed the musty coolness that is the smell of wet earth. How could that be? Following his nose, Benedict lowered his head to the ground and noticed that just below the stones on which he had been praying all night, there was moisture.

Startled, he moved a few rocks and dug an inch into the soil. There was no doubt: water was seeping up through the earth! Giving thanks to God, Benedict woke Placid, and the two solemnly placed three rocks beside each other to mark the place. Then they carefully made their way down the mountain to the cave, and slept the remaining hour or two until full dawn.

When the monks returned at mid-day, Benedict simply told them to climb back up the mountain and look themselves for the signs of God's presence there. He felt sure that God's power would pour forth to satisfy their need. When they went up and saw Benedict's three stone markers, they noticed a gathering pool of water below. Digging away the ground nearby, the monks found water filling up the hole faster than they could dig. They sang and praised God and rejoiced. Even today a full stream flows from the top of the mountain into the ravine below! God's goodness and care relieved the monks of the hardship of their long climb, and allowed them to remain faithfully in their monastic homes!

Of the many stories Benedict told me, this is one of my favorites. It was a miracle, and yet how can we be surprised to find God upwelling in life-giving water? To Moses, God's power poured out through water, both at the Red Sea and at the rock-become spring in the midst of the Sinai Desert. Jesus received the Spirit's blessing in the water of the Jordan, where he was baptized by John. And Jesus promises to be within us as a spring of water gushing up to eternal life. With all the ways God is revealed in creation, water is a sure sign of overflowing abundance, God's self-giving to us.

TEARS OF THE HEART

A GREAT DEAL REMAINS to be told about my abbot's life, rich in stories of holy power. Benedict could peer into people's hearts even at a distance, and his monks well knew they could never get away with lying to him. Why, he even brought King Tortila to his knees by seeing right through the mischief of that brutal old tyrant. And Benedict was even-handed with rich and poor, Roman and barbarian—everyone. He was especially tender to those in need. When the harvests were inadequate, poor farmers could always get food at Benedict's monastery; God seemed to bless Benedict by always providing enough for his monks, even when they had given everything away!

Benedict saw and loved Christ's presence in everyone, but if there was anyone who had a special place in his heart, it was his twin sister, Scholastica. The two had been close as children, and when they were just twelve years old, Benedict earnestly supported her decision to adopt the consecrated life of a virgin rather than to marry. He knew she was a loving person, and that she desired to love God above all, even as fervently as he.

Scholastica continued to live in their family home, adopting a semi-secluded life, turning away from fine clothes and jewelry and the social demands that normally would have been expected of her. Benedict's tutor taught both of them to read and write, so that Scholastica could also study scripture and copy religious manuscripts. Although Scholastica was relieved of many household duties, she and her nurse-servant contributed by spinning and weaving and working in the enclosed kitchen garden.

Since they had shared so much as children, it was especially difficult for the twins to be separated when Benedict went to Rome, and

through all his years in the cave at Subiaco, they
prayed for each other every day. Years passed
and the monasteries that Benedict founded grew
and flourished, and the time came for Benedict
to transfer his community to Monte Cassino,
south of Rome. Meanwhile, Scholastica had
also founded a community of women which was
growing and needed a new home too.

A noble Roman lady donated her summer
villa to the women. The villa was situated
close to Benedict's new monastery, on the
lower slopes of Monte Cassino. It was a lovely
place, with a well, an olive grove, grapevines
and beehives, and a modest number of goats,
geese and hens. Scholastica's community
found it a challenge to unite the daily rhythm
of prayer with the many tasks required to
maintain the farm, but they felt lucky to be
able to feed and clothe themselves mostly
from their own resources.

Although both Benedict and Scholastica
were busy with their own communities, they

met regularly to share problems and dreams. Each found strength from the other's encouragement of their vision of life in God's service, and both eagerly looked forward to their visits.

The particular visit I want to tell you about occurred when they were both beginning to show their age. The last few times Benedict had seen her, Scholastica had not been well, and he encouraged her to take regular baths and to eat meat. These were normally considered luxuries in those times, but Benedict felt baths and meat helped the sick regain strength and health. Sure enough, on our visit Scholastica was up and around, looking cheerful, even radiant. Benedict, along with me and a few of his disciples, had come to see her, and we spent the whole day singing God's praises and conversing about the spiritual life. As darkness began to fall, we sang the evening office of prayers together, and then ate a light meal of raw vegetables, stuffed olives and figs. No-one wanted to end the conversation, and we continued talking at table until it was quite late.

It was such joy to see the aging brother and sister together! Even now, they were like two peas in a pod, and their spiritual union was so pure that they could speak or be side-by-side in silence with equal ease.

Yet strangely, on this night, Scholastica did not want Benedict to leave. She spoke boldly to Benedict in the hearing of all of us: "Please do not leave me tonight brother. Your presence brings me such comfort, and I hate to let you go. Stay with me, talking about the joys of heaven, until the sun rises in the morning."

Well, our firm monastic custom is that we are to return to the monastery every night without exception, and the abbot always obeys the community rule with extra fidelity. Looking back now, we know that Scholastica must have had a premonition that her own death was near and wanted her brother's comfort

for a few more hours. But of course no-one knew it then.

Benedict was simply shocked that she of all people would ask him to break his rule, so his response was harsh. Quite abruptly, Benedict pulled back, "What are you saying, sister? How could you ask that I break the Rule of the monastery just to prolong our pleasure? It is completely impossible." Tears sprang into Scholastica's eyes, and she bent her head over her hands on the table. She seemed to be weeping, but also praying. As I watched her, it occurred to me that she was actually asking God to change her twin's mind. Astonishingly, the heavens responded to her grief and her need, and they too began to weep. Soon there was a ferocious thunderstorm, with heavy rain pouring down from skies which only a moment before had no cloud in sight! The great rainstorm prevented us from even setting a foot outside the door.

Benedict's first reaction was anger. He was intent on his purpose, and it seemed Scholastica was trifling with him. He shouted at her, "Woman, what have you done?" He was using exactly the same language by which Yahweh addressed Eve in the Garden of Eden, (Genesis 2:13). There was a shocked silence, for none of us could remember him *ever* speaking that meanly to *anyone*, much less his beloved sister. We all recognized the passage—including Scholastica, of course—and realized that in effect, he had just accused her of being the mother of sin! His own sister!

But surprise followed surprise on that extraordinary evening. To us, even more astonishing than Benedict's outburst, was Scholastica's serenity. She answered her brother simply and clearly: "When I appealed to you, you did not listen to me. So I turned to my God and He heard my prayer. You see, you cannot leave me now, even if you still wanted to." If the abbot's outburst had struck us dumb, even more so did this response. This humble woman had proved mightier in prayer than our abbot. In all the years of Benedict's mighty works of power, we had never seen anything like this.

To his credit, the old abbot said nothing, but simply sat down in wonder to consider what had happened. You know from all I have told you that Benedict always tried to learn from his mistakes. And he saw that he must have made a mistake here.

In our awed silence that evening, Benedict wondered why God would do such a thing: choose Scholastica's whim over his duty. As he pondered, he realized that his wish apparently had been contrary to that of God in this matter, while his sister's wish had been in harmony with God. Scholastica had been so looking forward to Benedict's visit, she found great joy in his presence and deeply desired the simple gift of a few more hours loving conversation about the joys of heaven that awaited her. Such deep love is the source of the greatest power in prayer. Even if she were sinning, Scholastica could be serenely confident at the response our Christ gives to the sinful woman in the gospels who appeals to Him for mercy: "Her many sins are forgiven, for she loved much." (Luke 7:36-50) Though he knew better, Benedict had allowed his heart to be cramped by concentrating on duty for its own sake, whereas Scholastica's heart grew greater with the inexpressible sweetness of love.

Duty is not a bad thing, but it must be applied flexibly in the service of charity. Benedict saw clearly that no rule alone can save us, although at times a little strictness is required. But the heart of the consecrated life is a loving relationship with God, involving devotion and tenderness not only towards the Creator but also to all God has created. No wonder Scholastica's tears had resounded in heaven!

In that moment, Benedict loved his sister all the more for what she had reminded him about God, and he saw how wonderfully pure her spirit had grown in love. He turned to Scholastica in sorrow and asked her forgiveness. "I will now certainly do your will and God's. Let us keep vigil together this night, praying and praising and speaking of heaven's joys all this night long." He hugged his sister warmly, and spent the entire night deriving great profit from the holy thoughts they exchanged.

When Benedict left her the next morning, his spirit was much in tune with hers, and both of them with God's Spirit. Scholastica died only a few days later, but her brother's heart was so in harmony with hers that at the moment of her death he looked up and saw his sister's soul leaving her body and penetrating the secret places of heaven in the form of a dove. He was overjoyed by the glory surrounding her, and gave thanks to God for her life and her safe passage to heaven. He rejoiced in the many gift she had given to his life, and he never forgot the wisdom of her gift of love. Benedict sent his monks to bring her body for burial in his own tomb, so that in death as in life, they would be united in God.

UNCREATED LIGHT

MY FAVORITE IMAGE OF Benedict is that of radiant light penetrating darkness. I got that image from an incident that occurred just a few weeks after Scholastica's death, and not long before Benedict's own. Benedict was a changed man after his sister died. Both souls had always been one in God, and he knew that would continue even though she had already crossed over. But now the difference in Benedict showed: it was as if she were so much a part of him that somehow his soul was already with her in the divine country...I cannot really explain it. He was gentler than ever and more loving, present to us as always, but at the same time more wrapped in God. This incident of the light made the change visible to all of us.

The Abbot Servandus, Benedict's old friend from the monastery at Campania, had come to visit him. Servandus and Benedict shared intimate talks about the truths of eternity, just as Benedict and Scholastica had done. Servandus arrived that day without fanfare, escorted simply by a few monks and a donkey, and had settled in the guest room below Benedict's cell. After evening prayers and supper, the two old abbots met, and for some long hours spoke together of their hopes and longings, tasting in advance the heavenly food that was not yet fully theirs to enjoy. At last they retired for the night, but Benedict could not sleep, so he arose again to pray.

Standing at the window in the deep night, Benedict gazed out in love upon the familiar moonlit landscape. All at once he beheld a flood of light breaking through the night's darkness, shining down through the sky. The light was more brilliant than the sun, obliterating every trace of darkness in its path. It was not the usual morning's gradual dawning, but a sudden night-time fullness of light, richer

and denser than anything Benedict had ever seen. Awestruck, the holy monk gazed in wonder at this light, and as he did so another remarkable sight followed. The light gathered into itself all the world. It was as if the universe was drawn together within the single powerful beam. All creation was revealed, enfolded in the light of God, as if Christ's own glory was embracing every creature to reveal its natural beauty!

Uplifted in joy, Benedict saw the whole universe at a glance, all the cities and people, forests and animals, time and space, all wrapped within the embracing radiance of that marvelous ray of light. It seemed to Benedict that he himself had slipped into the fullness of infinity and was being held within the heart and mind of God, seeing as God sees, loving as God loves, in union with all things as God is.

How long he stood there, enrapt, Benedict did not know. Then in the midst of this glorious vision, something else happened. He saw the soul of the bishop of Capua being carried up into heaven. At that point, he gathered his wits and called out to his friend Servandus to come and watch this marvel with him. Servandus hurried upstairs just in time to catch a glimpse of the miraculous light. He too was astonished as Benedict described to him what he had seen. The abbots sent a monk right away to find out if the bishop of Capua had indeed died, and later when they were told it was so, they were confirmed in their certainty that the gift of light was a true vision from God.

Several days later, when Benedict and Servandus told us what had happened, I exclaimed to my abbot: "But Lord Abbot, such things should happen to *you* because you are a saint!" He firmly answered, "Brother, I would consider it foolish indeed to cling to such a gift as if it were mine alone. The vision of light was given to me for sharing among us all, so that each of us might meditate on the certainty that God is in this place!" He urged us all to pray about the nature of the gift that his vision brought to every one of us. And you know, at first I could not find anything there for me, thinking myself unworthy. But the more I prayed, the more I saw that God meant to speak to me too, through my abbot.

—What, do you imagine, does it mean, that the whole world is gathered up in a single ray of light?—

I like the concreteness of the images. Benedict found the fullness of God, not by leaving behind the material world, but rather in an increased appreciation of the physical world. Looking with God's eyes, as it were, Benedict felt the truth behind all creation: that every single bit of life reveals something of the divine. Benedict used to insist that the kitchen pots and the garden tools were as precious as the vessels of the altar, if we only knew what we were seeing. That sacredness in the ordinary was doubly true of people; he said every person revealed something of Christ, if we knew how to look and love. So it was not really a surprise that in his most sublime moment, Benedict saw ordinary things in an extraordinary way. God did not take the place of the world, but showed even worldly things as they truly are in God's love.

It is so typical of Benedict to see ordinary things transformed. I think, above all, I learned from his vision that I too am meant to be transformed in God's love. Looking back on it, as I often have, I realize that my abbot usually saw me as I really am in God's eyes, as God meant me to be. And what God wanted for our life together was that we share daily practices intended to help us grow into our true selves. Or maybe our days were supposed to be structured so that we could grow a bigger and bigger place inside ourselves so God could live there. Whatever else Benedict's vision meant, it was a celebration of the goodness of life as given by God.

Light is a wonderful image for Benedict's way of living in God, isn't it? How wonderful that even a little light vanquishes the darkness, and shows things as they really are. How mysterious is the play of light and shadow in a fireplace. I am always amazed when the fire penetrates a log so completely that I cannot tell where the flame ends and the log begins. In that moment of complete union, the log is like our lives filled up with the flame of God's love. And that is what Benedict wanted for every one of us. May it be so.

Ω